The Elephants Dance!

Written and Illustrated by G. Lubbers

Dedicated to my grandson, Thomas

Check out the sing-a-long
guide at the back of the book

And the elephants dance,
boom, boom, boom, da- da, boom, boom, boom
boom, boom, boom, da- da, boom, boom, boom
boom, boom, boom, da- da, boom, boom, boom

And the elephants dance and jump and hop, up and down

And the elephants dance,
boom, boom, boom, da-da, boom, boom, boom
boom, boom, boom, da-da, boom, boom, boom
boom, boom, boom, da-da, boom, boom, boom

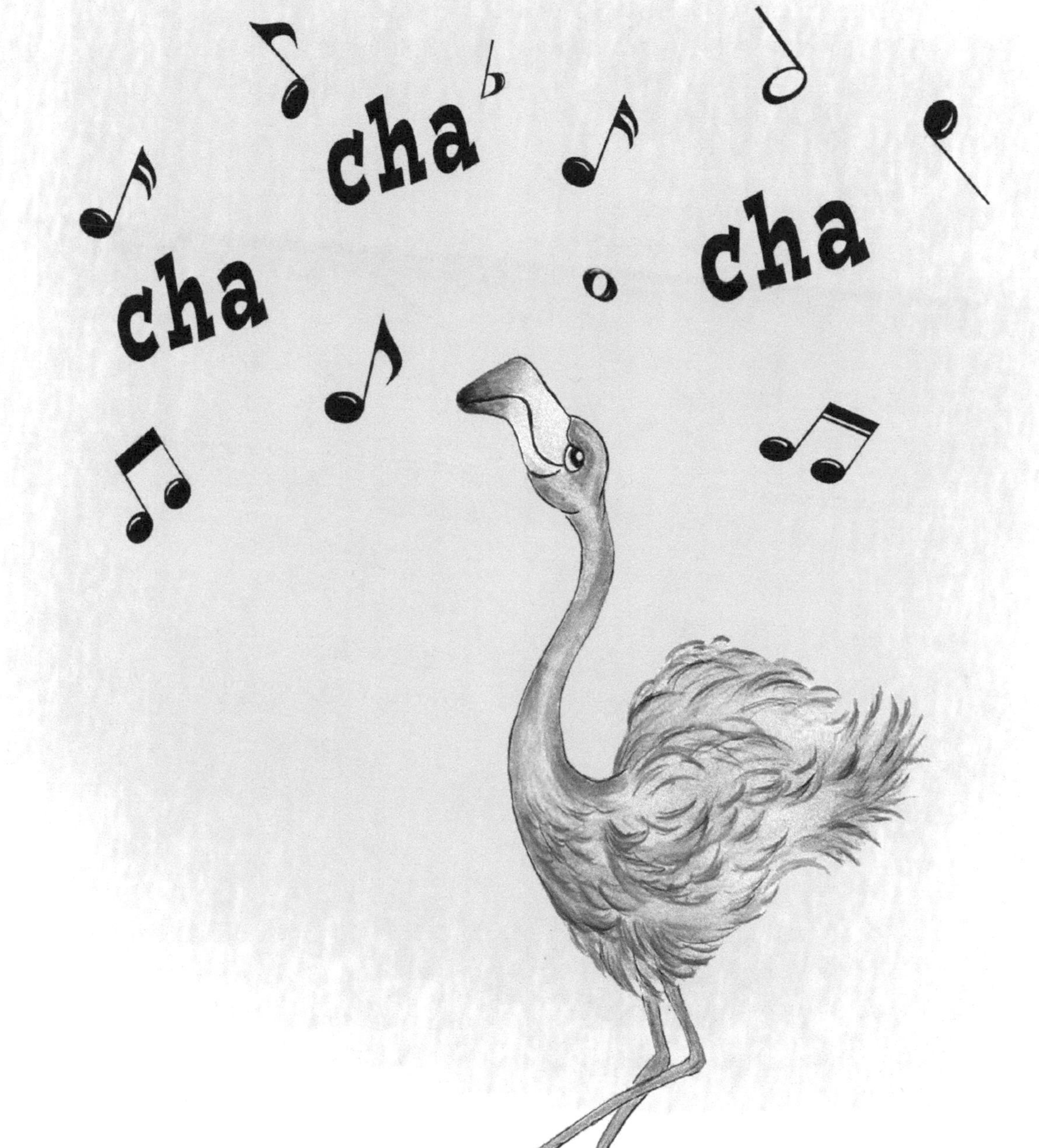
cha
cha
cha

And the elephants dance,
boom, boom, boom, da- da, boom, boom, boom
boom, boom, boom, da- da, boom, boom, boom
boom, boom, boom, da- da, boom, boom, boom

And the elephants dance and jump and hop, up and down

And the elephants dance and twirl and skip, 'round and 'round

and the elephants dance and hop...

DANCE!

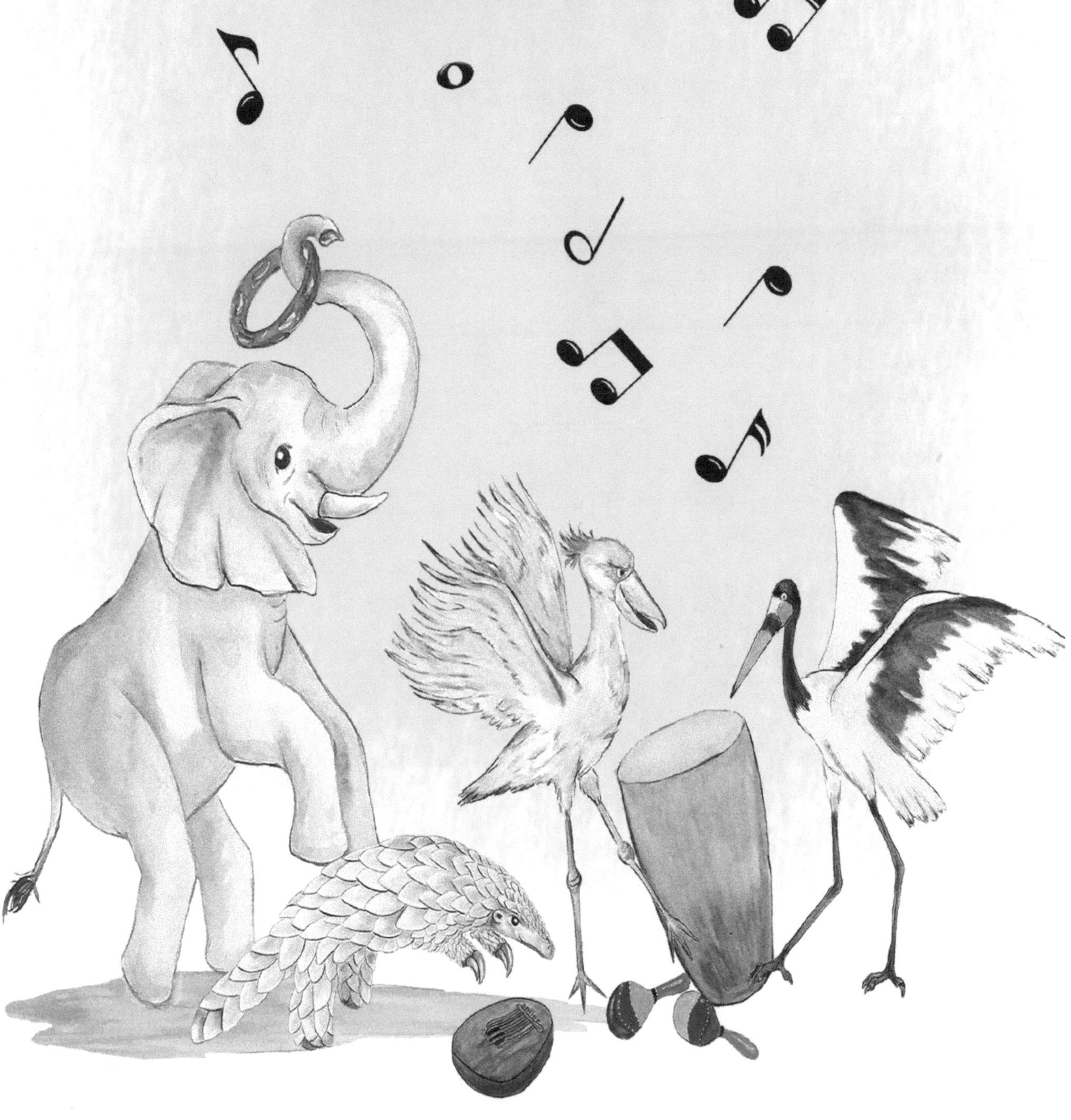

The hippos splash in the water
The giraffes nod to the beat (Clap your hands and count, "1, 2, 3")
The lion roars to the music, Roar! (Now it's your turn to roar out loud!)
The zebras stomp their feet (Now stomp your feet)

And the elephants dance. (It's time to dance and sing)
"Boom, boom, boom, da, da, boom, boom, boom"
"Boom, boom, boom, da, da, boom, boom, boom"

And the elephants dance and jump and hop, up and down. (Now hop up on down)
And the elephants dance and twirl and skip, 'round and 'round. (Now skip around and around)

And the elephants dance. (It's time to dance and sing)
"Boom, boom, boom, da, da, boom, boom, boom"
"Boom, boom, boom, da, da, boom, boom, boom"

The baboons drum on the tree trunk (Clap your hands on the top of your legs)
the meerkats hop up and down (Now hop up on down)
The flamingos dance on the water, Cha, Cha, Cha (Clap your hands above your head and sing, "Cha, Cha, Cha")
The cheetahs purr to the sound (Can you purr out loud?)

And the elephants dance. (It's time to dance and sing)
"Boom, boom, boom, da, da, boom, boom, boom"
"Boom, boom, boom, da, da, boom, boom, boom"

And the elephants dance and jump and hop, up and down. (Now hop up on down)
And the elephants dance and twirl and skip, 'round and 'round. (Now skip around and around)

And the elephants dance. (It's time to dance and sing)
"Boom, boom, boom, da, da, boom, boom, boom"
"Boom, boom, boom, da, da, boom, boom, boom"

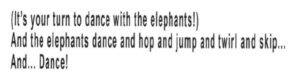

(It's your turn to dance with the elephants!)
And the elephants dance and hop and jump and twirl and skip...
And... Dance!

(Now shout, "boom, boom, boom!")

CPSIA information can be obtained
at www.ICGtesting.com
Printed in the USA
JSHW011403041119
2240JS00001B/3